The Boy and the Devil

The Boy
and the Devil

adapted from a Norwegian folktale and illustrated

by ERICA MAGNUS

 Carolrhoda Books, Inc., Minneapolis

For Peter

LIBRARY OF CONGRESS CATALOGING-IN-PUBLICATION DATA

Magnus, Erica.
  The boy and the devil.

  Summary: A retelling of the traditional Norwegian tale of how a little boy outwits the Devil.
  [1. Folklore—Norway] I. Title.
PZ8.1.M26Bo 1986 398.2′1′09481 [E] 86-14752
ISBN 0-87614-305-2 (lib. bdg.)

1 2 3 4 5 6 7 8 9 10 96 95 94 93 92 91 90 89 88 87 86

ne fine fall day a boy was walking through the forest looking for nuts when he came upon one that was worm-eaten. In spite of the hole, he decided to keep it and stuck it in his pocket.

By and by he met a stranger.

"Good day, little boy," said the stranger.

"Good day," said the boy politely.

Then he saw the black horse's
hoof, and the boy knew that here
was that old trickster himself!

"Is…is…is it true, what they say?"
he asked. "Can you really make
yourself as big as an elephant?"
"Oh, of course," replied the devil.

"Or...or as little as a flea?" added the boy hastily.

"Oh, of course," answered the devil.

"Can you creep into this little nut for me?" pleaded
the boy in his sweetest voice. "Oh please do it, oh please...."

So the devil crept into the nut.

As quickly as he could, the boy stuck a twig in the hole.

"Ah-ha!" he cried. "NOW I've got you!"

And with the devil safely in his pocket,

he went on his way.

By and by the boy came to a
blacksmith's shop.

"Can you crack this little nut for
me?" he asked the blacksmith.

"Oh, of course," said the man.
He placed the nut on his anvil
and gave it a whack with his
smallest hammer.

"YAAGH!" cried out the nut as it flew off the anvil.

"That is the *strangest* thing I have *ever* seen," remarked the puzzled blacksmith.

Again he placed the nut on the anvil and, taking a much larger hammer, gave it an even bigger whack.

"YEAAAUUGGH!!" screamed the nut as it hurled itself across the shop.

The blacksmith trembled with rage.

"This just cannot *be!* NO LITTLE NUT CAN GET THE BETTER OF ME!!" he bellowed, and, taking his largest sledge hammer, he hit the nut with all his might.

"YEEAAAUUUGGH!!!"

The blow was so great that the nut crashed through the roof, smashing it to pieces, and the walls came tumbling down.

Now the blacksmith was *VERY* shaken.

"I think," he said, quaking, "that the devil himself was in that nut!"

"Yes," said the boy, "he was."